D0462586

Have a Good Trip, MR. BEAN!

Based on the motion picture screenplay
by Hamish McColl and Robin Driscoll

PRICE STERN SLOAN
Published by the Penguin Group
Penguin Group (USA) Inc., 375 Hudson Street, New York, New York 10014, U.S.A.
Penguin Group (Canada), 90 Eglinton Avenue East, Suite 700, Toronto,
Ontario, Canada M4P 2Y3
(a division of Pearson Penguin Canada Inc.)
Penguin Books Ltd, 80 Strand, London WC2R 0RL, England
Penguin Ireland, 25 St Stephen's Green, Dublin 2, Ireland
(a division of Penguin Books Ltd)
Penguin Group (Australia), 250 Camberwell Road, Camberwell, Victoria 3124,
Australia (a division of Pearson Australia Group Pty Ltd)
Penguin Books India Pvt Ltd, 11 Community Centre, Panchsheel Park,
New Delhi - 110 017, India
Penguin Group (NZ), 67 Apollo Drive, Mairangi Bay, Auckland 1311,
New Zealand (a division of Pearson New Zealand Ltd)
Penguin Books (South Africa) (Pty) Ltd, 24 Sturdee Avenue, Rosebank,
Johannesburg 2196, South Africa

Penguin Books Ltd, Registered Offices:
80 Strand, London WC2R 0RL, England

www.mrbeansholiday.net

Library of Congress Control Number: 2006038107

ISBN 978-0-8431-2521-4   10 9 8 7 6 5 4 3 2 1

Have a Good Trip, MR. BEAN!

Based on the original character created by
Rowan Atkinson and Richard Curtis

Based on the motion picture screenplay by
Hamish McColl and Robin Driscoll

A Price Stern Sloan Junior Novel

PSS!
PRICE STERN SLOAN

Patter. Patter. Patter.

Raindrops pelted the streets of London.

Swoosh! The wind blasted through the air.

BOOM!

A crash of thunder rattled the city. It had rained so much for so long that the people of London were starting to forget what the sun looked like. The rain kept coming and coming, and the puddles kept getting bigger and bigger. There was enough water to make holes in the roof of a building, and there was indeed one such building, a church, with so many holes in its roof that buckets had to be placed all over the floor. That's why today this church was having a raffle to raise money for a new roof. It had to be rebuilt—and fast!

Putt . . . putt . . . putt. A tiny Mini car pulled into the church's parking lot. A man in a soaked tweed coat got out, sloshed through the rain, and entered the church.

"And now for our magnificent first prize!" the priest announced, pointing to a poster behind him. There was a stir of excitement in the crowd—the sunny beach scene was unlike anything anyone had seen in a long time.

"The winner of tonight's raffle will spend three glorious days on the beaches of the French Riviera," the priest continued. "You'll be staying in the beautiful city of Cannes, at the height of its world-famous film festival. And to top it all off, the winner will receive a magnificent new video camera perfect for recording every sun-filled moment of this fantastic vacation!"

The audience members clutched their raffle tickets, but no one clutched his more tightly than a man in the back. A man looking at the poster with longing. The owner of the

Mini car. A man named Mr. Bean.

"And the winner is number 919!" announced the priest.

Mr. Bean looked down at his ticket. Rats! The number on the ticket plainly and clearly read number 616. Mr. Bean sighed and dropped the useless ticket. It landed in the freight car of a model train that a little boy was playing with.

Moments passed and still no one had come up to claim the prize. The audience started to get bored. The little boy playing with the train set flicked the switch to turn it on. **Chugga-Chugga-Chugga**. The train started to move—taking Mr. Bean's ticket along for the ride. Mr. Bean stared as the train wound around the track, turning his ticket upside down. *It couldn't—no—but wait!* he thought. His number 616 ticket was also the number 919 ticket! Mr. Bean had won the trip!

"Does anybody have the number 919 ticket?" asked the priest. "Anybody? This is your last chance to claim a relaxing vacation at the beach."

A hand holding a very important ticket shot into the air and Mr. Bean began walking to the front of the room. It was his lucky day!

The next day, Mr. Bean packed. He fiddled with his new video camera, trying to figure out how it worked. Mr. Bean didn't even notice that he had turned it on. He plopped the camera on the table, and this is what it filmed:

A passport. A rolled-up beach towel. A pair of flippers and a snorkel. A mess of packaging, wires, and material from the box the camera came in.

Across the kitchen, Mr. Bean opens the freezer and pulls out a box of frozen fish sticks. He dumps it on the kitchen table, frozen fish sticks flying all over the kitchen and skidding across the floor. Then he finds what he is looking for: a wad of frozen money, hidden within the fish sticks.

WHIIRRRRVVVVVVVRRRRRRRR! *A hair dryer hovers over the frozen cash. Mr. Bean props the hair dryer up with the towel so that it can defrost, then dry, his hidden savings. He sits at the table with a folding board from a board game, a pot of glue, and travel brochures. He snips. He pastes. He folds the board back up. Now he has a map to take on his trip.*

One more thing to do before Mr. Bean can leave. He props Teddy in an armchair, facing a cardboard box with a TV screen drawn on it. Now Teddy will be entertained while Mr. Bean is away. Mr. Bean even makes Teddy a little remote control so that he doesn't have to watch the same channel day and night. Mr. Bean sighs—he wishes he could bring

*Teddy with him, but he only has one
ticket.*

*The film wobbles as Mr. Bean grabs
the camera and his suitcase and jogs
down the stairs. The door is open. The
rain is still pouring. Out the door—into
the rain—down the path—there's the
Mini—the suitcase in the trunk and
the camera in the front. Mr. Bean
slides into the driver's seat. He's ready
to go—as soon as he gets some video
footage of his departure. He backs the
Mini into the street, making sure to film
his house as he—***LOOK OUT FOR THAT BUS!
BEEEEEEEEEEEEEEEEPPPP!***

*The camera falls to the floor of the car
and bounces around as the car swerves.
Then Mr. Bean sets off at top speed. Stop-
go-stop-go-***SCREEEECH!*** "Watch where you're
going!" an angry voice yells.*

Now the camera stops bouncing around

as the car slows, then stops. Mr. Bean gets out of the car. He grabs the camera. He grabs his bag.

Before him is the train station.

Mr. Bean is on his way!

chapter 2

A few hours later, Mr. Bean was settled into a cushioned seat on the train, staring out the window as the French countryside zoomed past. He pulled out the game board. A homemade map was pasted to the center of the board, with a red line drawn from London to Paris to Cannes. That was the route Mr. Bean was taking to Cannes, where he would find the beautiful beach and relaxing holiday he needed. A blue line from Cannes to Paris to London marked Mr. Bean's trip home. By his calculations, the trip would take about nine hours each way. That meant that Mr. Bean had eighty-four hours of sunny paradise in store!

When Mr. Bean arrived in Paris, he would need to get from the *Gare du Nord* train station to the *Gare de Lyon* train station to catch his connecting train. But for now, he was thirsty. In the dining car, a smiling woman behind the counter greeted him.

"Bonjour!" she trilled in French.

Mr. Bean pointed at a picture of a cup of coffee.

"Un café?" the woman said, asking Mr. Bean if he wanted some coffee.

"Oui," Mr. Bean replied, trying out one of the French words he knew.

"Du sucre?" asked the woman, shaking a packet of sugar at Mr. Bean.

"Non," said Mr. Bean, trying out the *other* French word he knew.

"You speak excellent French!" the woman said in English as she handed Mr. Bean his coffee on a tray.

"Gracias," replied Mr. Bean with a grin—not realizing that he was saying "thank you" in *Spanish*. With the tray in his hands, Mr. Bean gave the train door a quick karate kick to open it. **Whoosh** parted the doors. Mr. Bean wobbled

down the aisle of the speeding train.

Slam! Mr. Bean fell into a row of seats as the train lurched to the left. His coffee sloshed in the cup. Mr. Bean regained his balance before the coffee spilled all over a woman reading a magazine. He sighed with relief.

A few steps later, the train lurched again. **Wham!** This time, Mr. Bean managed to stay upright—but he couldn't keep the coffee in its cup. The entire cup spilled into a sleeping businessman's open laptop.

Zzzzzzap! The laptop's screen went black!

A look of horror crossed Mr. Bean's face. He had to get away fast—before the businessman woke and found out what he'd done! Quietly and quickly, Mr. Bean closed the laptop and hurried down the aisle.

Then he stopped. He stared at his empty coffee cup. Mr. Bean had really wanted that cup of coffee. It seemed a shame to let it go to waste.

Mr. Bean crept back to the sleeping

businessman. He picked up the laptop and poured coffee from the keyboard into his cup. He gulped down his recycled coffee. Delicious!

Then the sleeping man began to stir. Now Mr. Bean really had to make a quick getaway. He slipped his empty cup into another sleeping passenger's hand and scrambled down the aisle.

Safely in the next car, Mr. Bean peeked through the glass to see what was happening. He'd escaped just in time. "Look what you've done!" the businessman shouted angrily at his seatmate. He pointed at the spilled coffee and the crackling, sparking laptop.

"I did nothing!" yelled the other passenger.

The two passengers were still fighting when the train pulled into the *Gare du Nord* station. One passenger whacked the other with the laptop. It was such an exciting fight that Mr. Bean filmed them as he stepped off the train. He even filmed the policemen who came running to the scene.

Mr. Bean had to take a taxi to the *Gare*

de Lyon station to catch his next train. But first, he filmed the colorful characters and interesting sights:

A street performer plays the accordion. The haunting music fills the station. A beautiful woman passes by. She stops to put some money in the accordion case. The street performer plays a romantic tune for her.

The woman walks away.

Mr. Bean turned off his camera. He stood in line for a taxi and glanced at a movie poster while he waited. The poster read:

PLAYBACK TIME

A Carson Clay film
Starring Carson Clay
Written by Carson Clay
Produced by Carson Clay
Directed by Carson Clay
He broke the rules. She broke his heart.

Then a taxi pulled up. Mr. Bean showed the driver his game board map, pointing to the *Gare de Lyon*. The driver nodded. Mr. Bean turned away to pick up his suitcase and camera case. When he did, a businessman slipped into his taxi, and the taxi drove off!

A second taxi pulled up while Mr. Bean was still gathering his bags. Another businessman leaned in and asked to be taken to *La Defense*, a major office district in the heart of Paris.

The businessman reached down to pick up *his* bags. Mr. Bean jumped into the other man's cab, expecting to be taken to the *Gare de Lyon*. He had no idea where he was actually going . . . and that's when Mr. Bean's journey *really* began!

Mr. Bean stood in a vast, open square. Towering office buildings surrounded him. This place did *not* look like a train station. And he didn't see a single train.

He stopped a man heading toward the street. Mr. Bean did his best train impression. He moved his arms in circles like a train's wheels. **"Chugga-chugga-chugga-chugga-choo-choo!"** he said.

But the man shook his head and walked away.

Mr. Bean approached another stranger. This time, he put more energy into his train impression. He waved his arms in wider circles. He made louder train noises. **"CHUGGA-CHUGGA-CHUGGA-CHUGGA-CHOO-CHOO!"**

But this person looked a little afraid of Mr. Bean. He turned and ran the other way.

It was clear that no one was going to help Mr. Bean find the *Gare de Lyon*. He would have to figure it out for himself.

Mr. Bean found a large poster with a map of Paris on it. A red arrow pointed to *La Defense* to show where he was. He traced the map with his finger until he found the *Gare de Lyon*. Then Mr. Bean drew a straight line between the two. All he had to do was follow that line, and he'd be at the train station in no time.

Mr. Bean pulled his compass out of his pocket. He was sure that if he stared at it for the entire walk, he wouldn't lose his way.

Left foot. Right foot. Left foot. Right foot. Mr. Bean walked the streets of Paris in a straight line. He walked through a shrub. He walked over a bench. He walked into a bottle of water that toppled over, leaving a man on the bench with *very* wet pants.

Zoom! Cars sped down a busy road. Mr. Bean walked right through the middle of them.

Vrrrrroooom! More cars raced past, including a sleek, expensive black car. Inside the car, a little boy stared out the window at Mr. Bean—but Mr. Bean didn't notice.

With his eyes glued to his compass, Mr. Bean walked into a restaurant. At one table, a waiter showed off a strawberry tart from a dessert cart. The cart was in Mr. Bean's way, so he gave it a quick push and kept walking.

The waiter didn't see Mr. Bean push the cart away—and he dropped the tart on the floor! **Splat!** Another waiter slipped in the mess. **Squish!**

But Mr. Bean kept walking in a straight line, never looking up from his compass. He still didn't notice anything around him—not even the crowd of paparazzi, their flashing cameras, or the fancy limousine carrying Carson Clay!

"Mr. Clay! How long will you be staying in Paris?" yelled a reporter over Mr. Bean's head.

Carson Clay smiled as Mr. Bean walked in front of him. "I have an exciting new project in the south tomorrow, and then I'll be in Cannes for the premiere of my new film. *Merci!*"

Click! Click! Click! Photographers scrambled to snap a picture of the Hollywood star. But every shot captured Mr. Bean blocking Carson Clay's flashing grin.

Mr. Bean walked on, staring at his

compass. Finally, he looked up. A satisfied smile spread over his face.

The *Gare de Lyon* train station rose before him.

Mr. Bean had made it!

chapter 3

Mr. Bean walked into the station. He turned his camera on, and this is what he filmed:

People. People rushing across the marble floors. People dashing to catch a train. People hugging hello and kissing good-bye. All sorts of people at the train station for all sorts of reasons.

The Destination Board, with flashing lights and numbers and French words. The Destination Board, telling everyone which trains are coming into town.

The Departure Board. More flashing lights, more numbers, more French words. The Departure Board, telling everyone which trains are leaving—and when.

Zoom in for a close-up. The image blurs, then focuses on one line: CANNES: VOIE 1.

Mr. Bean's train—and it's leaving from Track 1!

The picture joggles and jiggles as Mr. Bean races to Track 1. He's got to make it on the train to Cannes—or he'll lose precious vacation hours sitting in the station!

Track 1 looms before Mr. Bean. A train rests, waits. Mr. Bean pants. He checks his watch. The train doesn't leave for a few more minutes. That leaves plenty of time for a snack!

Mr. Bean sauntered over to a vending machine near Track 1. Delicious-looking baguette sandwiches were for sale inside.

Mr. Bean licked his lips. All this traveling had made him hungry! He tried to decide which one to buy. The sausage and cheese sandwich looked particularly tasty!

Mr. Bean patted his pockets. Uh-oh—he didn't have any change. Luckily, there was a slot for bills on the machine. He glanced around warily to make sure no one was watching as he pulled the roll of defrosted cash from his pocket. Mr. Bean cupped his hands around the bills to hide them.

He did not realize that he was also holding the end of his tie.

Mr. Bean tried to slip a bill into the machine.

Slurp!

But the machine hadn't sucked up his money—it had sucked up the end of his tie instead!

Mr. Bean's eyes opened wide. His tie was being pulled into the machine, which meant that Mr. Bean was being pulled into the machine, too! He tugged the tie, trying to get it out of the machine. But it kept disappearing farther into the money slot. Mr. Bean braced his feet against the floor. He scrunched up his face. He used all his strength to yank back his tie.

Wham! Mr. Bean was slammed against the vending machine. There were only a few inches of his tie left between him and the machine. Soon Mr. Bean's head was pressed against the glass-and-metal machine. The buttons were making marks on his face.

Wheeeeeeet! A shrill whistle blared. Mr. Bean's train was about to leave. He had to get free from the vending machine—fast!

Suddenly, the end of his tie appeared out the rejected money slit. Mr. Bean had a brilliant idea. He could take off the tie and let it go through the machine! His fingers fumbled with the knot at his neck.

Wheeeeeeet! Wheeeeeeet! The train's whistle blew. Mr. Bean's ride was about to leave the station!

Mr. Bean frantically tore at his tie. Finally

the knot was loose enough for him to slip the tie over his head. He grabbed his bag and raced for the train . . .

Just as it pulled out of the station.

Mr. Bean sat on a hard wooden bench. Now that he had missed his train, he had to figure out what to do next. He glanced at the signs and posters around him. Nearby was an ad for yogurt, Fruzzi Yogurt. It was a strange ad, featuring Napoléon, a famous French emperor from long ago, happily eating a strawberry yogurt as his army was being defeated. Large letters beneath the ad read:

FOR BETTER OR WORSE: FRUZZI.

Mr. Bean frowned. Stupid ad. He was only interested in the Departure Board. The next train to Cannes left in an hour. With a sigh, Mr. Bean got out his itinerary. He crossed out the original hours he had listed for travel time and vacation time. Next, he updated his schedule:

Hours in Cannes: ~~84~~ 83
Travel time: ~~8~~ 9

Then Mr. Bean decided to look on the bright side. He was still hungry—and with an hour until the next train, he had time for a proper meal.

Mr. Bean ambled through the station until he found a restaurant called *Le Train Bleu*. He walked inside. A man in a tuxedo—the maître d'—suddenly appeared. *"Vous desirez déjeuner, monsieur? Je vous en prie!"* He had asked Mr. Bean if he wanted to eat lunch. With a simpering smile, he took Mr. Bean's arm and led him to a table in the center of the room. The maître d' presented Mr. Bean with a large menu. Mr. Bean's eyes lit up. He was hungry!

Then he opened the menu. It was written entirely in French—which made it useless!

The maître d' seemed to sense Mr. Bean's problem. *"En entrée, je vous propose un artichaut vinaigrette, et a suivre, un plateau de fruits de mer. Cela vous convient?"* suggested the maître d', hoping that Mr. Bean would enjoy an artichoke appetizer and a seafood platter.

Mr. Bean looked at the maître d' blankly.

"Oui?" prompted the maître d' smoothly.

"Oui!" replied Mr. Bean. He wasn't sure what he was agreeing to, but at least he recognized the word!

The maître d' bowed and disappeared. It wasn't long before the first course was ready. As Mr. Bean took out his camera, a waiter approached his table. He was carrying a tray with a small bowl of oily dressing and a lumpy, gray-green thing covered in spiky leaves.

Mr. Bean stared at the thing. He couldn't even tell what it was.

It was the artichoke—his appetizer— and Mr. Bean couldn't believe that anyone would want to eat that. But Mr. Bean was too hungry to be picky. He had to figure out how to eat that . . . thing. He looked around the room, trying to see if anyone else was eating one. A large man at the table behind Mr. Bean had an artichoke in front of him. Mr. Bean stared at him, and the man glared back. Mr. Bean turned around.

Then Mr. Bean had an idea. He could use the camera to film how the man behind him ate the artichoke—and the man would never know what Mr. Bean was doing! Mr. Bean turned the camera on and propped it up on the table. A few minutes later, he rewound the tape. This is what the camera had recorded:

The man tears a leaf off the artichoke. He dips the leaf in the bowl of vinaigrette. Then he—

A waiter walks into the scene. He pauses at the man's table. He moves away.

The man puts the artichoke leaf on a side plate.

Mr. Bean was confused. He watched the tape again. He didn't know that while the waiter was standing at the table, the man ate the artichoke and dressing out of each leaf. But on the tape, it looked like the man was simply dipping the leaf in dressing, then putting it on a plate.

Mr. Bean shrugged. If that was what he was supposed to do with the artichoke, he would do it! After all, when in France, do as the French do!

He tore off an artichoke leaf, dipped it in dressing, and promptly dropped it on an extra plate. Then he did it again. And again. The people in the restaurant were staring at him in disbelief.

Growl! This wasn't doing anything for Mr. Bean's grumbling stomach!

The waiter swooped in again, bearing the *fruits de mer*—a bowl of crushed ice with six quivering oysters and five small lobsters. Mr. Bean looked at the bowl. The lobsters seemed to be looking back at him.

Mr. Bean picked up his spoon and started digging around in the ice. He wasn't sure where his food was. Surely he wasn't supposed to eat the slimy gray oysters? Or the beady-eyed lobsters? Well, there was always the ice. Mr. Bean crunched down on a large spoonful of it. Ice wasn't very flavorful. But at least it didn't have beady black eyes.

From across the room, the maître d' saw Mr. Bean chowing down on the ice. He raced over. *"Monsieur, les huîtres aussi sont delicieuses!"* he exclaimed, placing a delicious oyster in front of Mr. Bean.

Mr. Bean picked up the oyster's shell. **Squ-u-elch!** He dropped the oyster into his mouth. It was salty, slimy, cold, and clammy—in a word, horrible. Mr. Bean shuddered and made a terrible face as the oyster slid down his throat. Ugh! He would never eat another one of *those* again!

Mr. Bean pretended to slurp down the oysters in rapid succession. But he was really pouring them into the napkin in his lap! As soon as the maître d' turned away, Mr. Bean dumped the oysters into the handbag of the woman sitting behind him.

The maître d' swooped past again. *"Monsieur, vos langoustines!"* He prompted Mr. Bean to try one of the small lobsters. Mr. Bean stared at the creepy-looking creature, with its pinkish-red shell, pinching claws, scrawny legs, and beady eyes. He took a deep breath—and popped the lobster in his mouth, shell, claws, and all! **Crunch!**

A woman outside the restaurant stopped and stared at Mr. Bean through the window, the lobster's claws still hanging out of his mouth. It was the beautiful woman he had seen earlier while he had filmed the street musician.

Mr. Bean gulped down the lobster. Suddenly, the phone rang in the handbag behind Mr. Bean—the same handbag where he had hidden the nasty oysters! A look of horror crossed Mr. Bean's face. He frantically waved his arm in the air, trying to get the waiter's attention. He had to get out of the restaurant—*now*.

As the woman reached for her bag, Mr. Bean jumped up from the table. He quickly walked up the aisle. He had almost reached the door when—

"**Ahhhhhhhhhhhhhhhhhhhhhhhhhhhhhhhhhhhhhhh!**"

The woman had grabbed a handful of oysters out of her purse!

It was just as well that Mr. Bean had hurried out of *Le Train Bleu* when he did— his train to Cannes was leaving in a few minutes. But first, Mr. Bean wanted some video footage of him boarding the train. He stopped a handsome man who was carrying a cup of coffee and a can of juice. What Mr. Bean didn't know was that the man was the famous Russian film director Emil Dachevsky.

"Could you . . . ?" Mr. Bean asked, pointing at his camera.

Emil was in a hurry. He didn't want to film Mr. Bean, but he agreed to do it anyway. He carefully placed the coffee and juice on the platform next to the train and took Mr. Bean's camera.

Mr. Bean gave Emil a thumbs-up and began to board the train—just as a long luggage cart stretched in front of the shot. Mr. Bean shook his head. That was *not* the footage he wanted. They'd have to try again!

TAKE TWO:

Mr. Bean waved at Emil to start filming again. He walked up to the train—and kicked over Emil's coffee!

Now Emil was really getting annoyed. Mr. Bean apologized and moved the can of juice out of the way so that he wouldn't knock that over on the next take.

TAKE THREE:

Mr. Bean strode up the platform and stepped onto the train. From the doorway, he waved at the camera.

Perfect!

Emil handed Mr. Bean the camera and turned to get the can of juice.

SLAM!

The train doors closed!

Mr. Bean watched as Emil dropped the juice and ran up to the train. He banged on the windows furiously. The train's engine began to rumble. It began to inch out of the station. Emil started screaming and shouting in Russian. It was such a sight that Mr. Bean decided to film it.

"Papa!"

Lowering the camera, Mr. Bean looked into the train car. He was horrified to see a small boy banging on the window—just like the man outside!

"Papa! Papa! What's happening? What should I do?" shouted the boy in Russian.

As the train picked up speed, Emil tore down the platform next to it. "Stefan! Next stop! Get out at the next stop!" he yelled desperately.

And with that, the train zoomed out of the station. In moments, Emil was only a dot on the platform.

The boy, Stefan, was the same one who'd been watching Mr. Bean from the window of the black car. He buried his head in his hands and tried not to cry. Mr. Bean awkwardly sat down across from him. He gave Stefan a little smile.

But Stefan didn't smile back. Instead—slap—he whacked Mr. Bean across the face!

Mr. Bean toppled into the aisle. Grumbling, he crawled to the back of the car and pulled himself into a seat. He rubbed his cheek and glared at Stefan. It was just his luck to be stuck with a bratty little kid.

Soon the conductor arrived in the car.

"Billets, s'il vous plaît. Billets, s'il vous plaît," he called in French as he punched each passenger's ticket. When the conductor reached Stefan, the little boy pointed at Mr. Bean. Stefan didn't have a ticket of his own. It was still with his father, stuck on the train platform!

The conductor headed straight for Mr. Bean, expecting to collect two tickets. But Mr. Bean had only one ticket—for himself. He handed his ticket to the conductor.

"Et l'autre, monsieur," demanded the conductor, holding his hand out for Stefan's ticket.

Mr. Bean patted his pockets, pretending to look for the other ticket. He pointed at the pile of suitcases, trying to convince the conductor that the other ticket was in his bag. The conductor moved aside to let Mr. Bean look in his suitcase.

Mr. Bean spotted a businessman engrossed in his work. There was a ticket on the table next to the man's laptop. While the conductor's back was turned, Mr. Bean strode up to the man. *"Billet,"* he droned in an impression of the conductor.

Without looking up, the man handed Mr. Bean his ticket! **Click!** Mr. Bean clicked his tongue in his mouth to make the noise of the ticket punch. Then he handed the businessman his own ticket—the one that had already been punched. The businessman didn't notice a thing!

Mr. Bean sauntered back down the aisle and handed the conductor the ticket he'd taken from the businessman. As the man punched it, Mr. Bean settled into his seat, feeling very satisfied with himself.

Soon the train rolled to a stop as it pulled into the next station. While the unfortunate businessman was being kicked off for not having a good ticket, Mr. Bean glanced up to see Stefan bolt off the train. Mr. Bean was glad he didn't have to worry about him anymore. He watched little Stefan sitting by himself in the big, empty station and sighed. It didn't seem right to leave him all alone. Mr. Bean stepped off the train.

But it was *his* holiday! He shouldn't have to waste any more of it watching over some brat who had slapped him in the face! As the train whistle blew, Mr. Bean stepped back on the train. He waved at Stefan.

And that's when Mr. Bean noticed Stefan filming him—with his own camera! He jumped off the train and ran for his camera—just as the doors slammed shut behind him.

Mr. Bean turned around in horror. There, sitting in the luggage rack, was his suitcase!

Stefan had the camera running, and this is what he filmed:

The train starts to move. Mr. Bean starts to run. The train picks up speed. So does Mr. Bean. Mr. Bean bangs on the windows. He screams. He shouts. But the train just moves faster and faster. Mr. Bean does, too, until he falls off the end of the platform!

Mr. Bean picks himself up and climbs back onto the platform. The train zooms into the distance. Mr. Bean hops and jumps and dances with rage. He shakes his head, and he shakes his fists. He swings his arms in the air. He stares daggers at Stefan and into the camera.

Mr. Bean had never been so angry in his entire life!

chapter 4

Stefan waited patiently for Mr. Bean to stop dancing with rage. At last, Mr. Bean slumped onto the edge of the bench. He sat across from another strange yogurt ad: a group of French revolutionaries crowded around an aristocrat who was about to have his head cut off in a guillotine. But the aristocrat didn't seem to mind, as he was enjoying a raspberry-flavored yogurt. This time, the tagline read:

EVEN WHEN IT'S BAD, IT'S GOOD: FRUZZI.

But Mr. Bean wasn't interested in strange yogurt ads. He had to find out when the *next* train to Cannes would leave. He found the Departure Board. Mr. Bean emptied his pockets. He pulled out a cord for his camera, his wallet, his toothbrush, and his itinerary.

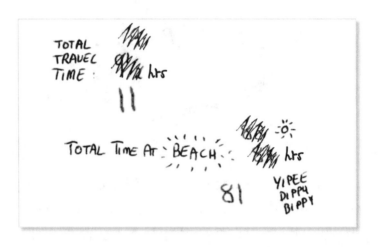

TOTAL
TRAVEL
TIME : ~~1~~ ~~1½~~ ~~9½~~ ~~8½~~ hrs

11

TOTAL TIME AT BEACH ~~18~~ ~~17~~ hrs ☀

81

YIPEE
DIPPY
BIPPY

Once again, he changed it: two hours less holiday time, two hours more journey time.

Since Mr. Bean seemed calmer, Stefan crept up to him. With a shy smile, he handed Mr. Bean his camera. Suddenly, Stefan looked down the platform.

The next train was approaching and it had to have Stefan's father on it! Mr. Bean and Stefan raced to meet the train. Emil was standing in the front car. But he didn't look excited or happy. Instead, a look of desperation crossed his face.

The train slowed down but didn't stop.

Emil was on an express train—he was going straight to the next station!

Emil banged furiously on the window as he held up a piece of cardboard. The cardboard had a cell phone number and the word CANNES written on it. Mr. Bean and Stefan ran as fast as they could to keep up with the train. Then Mr. Bean had a brilliant idea. He took his camera and filmed Emil's phone number.

The train zoomed through the station.

Emil was gone.

Mr. Bean quickly rewound the tape and watched what he had filmed.

The train zips backward into the station. Emil's panicked face appears. Zoom in on the numbers on the card.

PAUSE

The film freezes.

The numbers are easy to read. But Emil's

fingers cover the last two digits of the phone number.

Stefan stared at the screen of the camera. "I can't read the last two numbers!" he cried in Russian. On the back of Mr. Bean's itinerary, Stefan began writing a long list. 00, 01, 02, 03, 04, 05, 06 . . .

Finally Mr. Bean realized what Stefan was doing—writing down all the different combinations for the last two digits of the phone number! He grabbed the pen and itinerary from Stefan and started scribbling even faster—all the numbers from 00 to 99.

Mr. Bean and Stefan found a pay phone. They dialed the first number, and Stefan held the phone to his ear. "*'Allo?*" he said.

A woman in an office picked up her phone. "*'Allo?*" she asked.

Stefan shook his head. Onto the next number! Mr. Bean crossed out 00 from their list and dialed again.

A woman in a salon, her head covered in

strips of tinfoil, picked up her phone. *"'Allo?"* she said.

Stefan shook his head again. Mr. Bean crossed out 01 and dialed the next number. It was going to be a long afternoon.

But when Mr. Bean turned to hand the phone to Stefan, the little boy was no longer standing next to him. He glanced around the station and saw Stefan standing in the doorway of a train that had just arrived.

"Get on!" Stefan yelled in Russian, waving at Mr. Bean to join him. Mr. Bean ran across the platform and jumped onto the train just before its doors closed.

Suddenly, a look of horror crossed Mr. Bean's face. He slapped his hands on his pocket as he stared out the window.

His wallet was still on top of the pay phone!

Once again, Mr. Bean burst into his jumping dance of fury. Absolutely nothing was going right!

Stefan noticed the ticket inspector before Mr. Bean did. He ran up to Mr. Bean and hissed in Russian, "Ticket inspector!"

Mr. Bean smiled confidently. He knew how to handle this. He strode over to two men working on laptops. *"Billets!"* he said authoritatively.

The men looked up at Mr. Bean, confused. Why was this stranger asking for their tickets?

Mr. Bean tried to slink away. But the ticket inspector was approaching! Mr. Bean pushed Stefan into the gap between two seats, then tried to hide in the handicapped bathroom.

But the inspector found him anyway. And at the next station, he kicked Mr. Bean and Stefan off the train.

There was nothing to do but keep trying different phone numbers. There was just one little problem: Mr. Bean and Stefan didn't have any money! As Stefan checked the return-change slot in the pay phones, Mr. Bean noticed a row of closed-circuit security cameras. He was so frustrated with his vacation, he couldn't help making a few nasty faces at them, bulging his eyes and twisting his mouth.

A stationmaster frowned as he watched Mr. Bean. Stefan pulled Mr. Bean away from the cameras. Then he spotted a woman sitting on a bench and he winked at Mr. Bean as if to say *watch this*!

Stefan crept up to the woman. He made a tragically sad face. "Please help me. I'm trying to get money so I can see my dad," he implored in Russian.

The woman smiled indulgently and handed Stefan three coins!

But when Mr. Bean tried to follow Stefan's lead—speaking his best "Russian"—all he got was a nasty frown and a shake of the head as well as a look from the stationmaster. Mr. Bean and Stefan walked away. They were just going to have to find another way to make enough money for the bus fare. And they had to be quick. After all, Stefan had to get back to his father, and Mr. Bean needed to get to the beach!

Mr. Bean and Stefan settled in a deserted bus shelter for the night. Stefan curled up on the plastic bench to try to get some sleep. Mr. Bean got out a pen and changed his itinerary again.

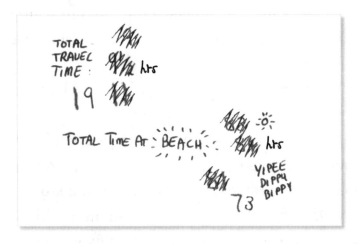

With his schedule updated, Mr. Bean decided to get ready for bed. He pulled a

Mr. Bean plots his course across Paris.

The shortest distance between two points is a straight line.

Mr. Bean gets stuck trying to get a snack.

Eww!

Aaah!

Mr. Bean has an idea . . .

When in doubt—dance!

Mr. Bean plays the part of a grieving mother—and gets a standing ovation!

"Here, chickychick!" calls Mr. Bean. One of these cluckers has his train ticket!

Still dancing . . .

Mr. Bean to the rescue!

The beautiful actress from
the yogurt commercial was
heading to Cannes, too!

Wanted!

Mr. Bean and Stefan sneak into the theater.

A quick getaway.

Finally— the beach!

toothbrush out of his pocket and walked over to a water fountain, but it was broken. Mr. Bean found a Coke machine and bought a can of sugary soda. He poured that on his toothbrush and starting brushing his teeth.

Stefan was fast asleep on the bench. Mr. Bean pulled his jacket over the boy to tuck him in. Then he closed his eyes. It had been a long day.

And who knew what tomorrow would bring?

chapter 5

BEEP! BEEP! HONK! HONK!

Mr. Bean opened one eye. He opened the other eye.

Bright sunlight was streaming through the bus shelter's windows. People were bustling around everywhere. A busy marketplace had sprung up right around him!

Mr. Bean rubbed his eyes and sat up. He looked over at Stefan—the little brat was still asleep. Mr. Bean shook him awake. Stefan opened his eyes, stretched, and jumped off the bench.

Mr. Bean and Stefan walked through the market, pausing at a crowd of people surrounding a group of street performers. When the musicians finished playing a song, the people clapped. They also threw money at them!

And that gave Mr. Bean an idea. Nearby, a music seller was playing CDs. All Mr. Bean had to do was wait for the next song . . .

Which just happened to be a lively Irish jig!

Mr. Bean started to jig, stomping his feet on the ground. He looked so ridiculous that Stefan couldn't bear to watch. No one else watched, either—and no one gave him any money.

A new song started to play—Shaggy's "Mr. Boombastic." Mr. Bean wiggled his hips and shimmied. It was even worse than the Irish jig!

Luckily for Mr. Bean, "Mr. Boombastic" soon ended and another song began. He lip-synched along with the new tune, a sad and dramatic opera about a grieving mother, called "O Mio Babbino Caro."

And people stopped to watch!

Mr. Bean ripped off his sweater and wrapped it around his head. He threw his arms around the squirming Stefan, who wanted nothing to do with this plan. Mr. Bean had become the grieving mother—with Stefan as the dying son!

Mr. Bean kept lip-synching, pausing to wail with sorrow. He winked at Stefan, who started playing along by dramatically pretending to die. The crowd grew bigger and bigger. Mr. Bean started wailing louder and louder. When the song ended, the crowd burst into applause—and showered coins and bills on Mr. Bean and Stefan! Mr. Bean grinned at Stefan. They were really on their way now!

In no time, Mr. Bean and Stefan were boarding a bus to Cannes. Mr. Bean carried two ice-cream cones and held his ticket in his mouth.

"Cannes, monsieur?" asked the driver after Stefan clambered aboard.

"Oui!" Mr. Bean proudly proclaimed. But the instant he opened his mouth, his ticket fluttered away on the breeze!

Mr. Bean shoved the cones at Stefan and took off after his ticket. *There*—Mr. Bean was about to grab it. But a woman walking by pierced it with her high-heeled shoe!

Mr. Bean kept his eyes on the ticket. As soon as it fell off her heel, it became stuck to the wheel of a baby carriage. He chased after the carriage until the ticket became unstuck from the wheel. *Finally* he was going to grab it—when a chicken stepped on it! **Cluck!** The chicken ran away from Mr. Bean's outstretched hands, carrying the ticket along with it!

Mr. Bean raced after the chicken. But a farmer scooped it up and caged it! Mr. Bean watched in horror as the cage was loaded onto a truck full of chickens. But he wasn't going to stop chasing that chicken—or his ticket. Nearby, an old man was repairing a bike. Mr. Bean grabbed the bike, tossed his camera in the basket, and took off.

Mr. Bean pedaled like a madman over the bumpy dirt road. His camera bounced in the basket. During all this bumping around, the camera was turned on, and this is what it recorded:

The road. The sky. The ground. The road. The ground. The sky. The truck. Mr. Bean's determined face.

The truck—farther away! A speeding SUV—the side of the road—back on the road. Seven bicyclists, one in a yellow jersey, all of them in the way!

Mr. Bean, pedaling faster and faster. The truck—nearer now—the chicken in its cage—the ticket on the floor—Mr. Bean's grin. His arm, reaching out—almost at the ticket—

WOOF! WOOF! WOOF! *A giant dog jumps out of nowhere! Mr. Bean jerks backward. The bike falls forward. The front wheel is off!*

Mr. Bean tilts the bike back. He balances on one wheel. He rides the broken bike like a unicycle. The other wheel rolls along next to him.

Mr. Bean bites his tongue and concentrates. He wobbles along the road. He balances the broken bike over the rolling wheel. Ready—steady—now! He drops the bike over the wheel. **CLICK!** *The bike has two wheels again!*

Back to the road. The truck slows. It stops at a barn. Mr. Bean pedals furiously. He knows he'll have his ticket again soon! He jumps off the bike and runs over to the barn.

Mr. Bean flung open the barn door, ready to find the chicken with his ticket. But there were hundreds—thousands—hundreds of thousands of chickens, clucking and pecking at the floor. And no sign of his ticket anywhere.

It would be impossible to find it among so many chickens!

Mr. Bean, grumbling, turned around to walk back to the bike. And what he saw in the street amazed him: the bike, flattened like a pancake!

Mr. Bean looked left. He looked right. *What could have happened to the bike?* He ran over to it and was relieved to find his camera unharmed. He rewound the tape to see if there were any clues.

The empty road. The seven cyclists pass by. The country road is quiet. Peaceful.

Then the film begins to jostle. The road is vibrating. A tank is approaching, and it runs right over the bike!

Mr. Bean looked down the road. A tank? Roaming the countryside? Mr. Bean was shocked. But he had even more things to worry about.

How was he going to get back to Stefan?

And how was he *ever* going to make it to the beach?

Mr. Bean stood by the side of the road, his arm out, his thumb up. **Whooosh.** One car passed. **Whooosh.** A second car passed. **Whooosh.** A third car passed.

Not one of them stopped.

With no cars stopping, Mr. Bean decided to have fun with his camera. He propped it on a rock and turned it on, and this is what was filmed:

Mr. Bean makes a goofy face at the camera. He hops down the road. He skips, he walks backward, he lollops around.

He sees a small wooden hut across the road. He steps inside to inspect it. **WHOOOSH! SLAM!** *A gust of wind shuts the door behind him—and it locks from the outside!*

Mr. Bean bangs on the door. **THUMP-THUMP-THUMP.** *But there is no one near to help him. He lifts the hut and totters* *down the road, weaving back and forth. He can't see a thing—not even the massive truck barreling down the road! He wanders offscreen, just ahead of the truck.*

HONK! HONK! SMASH!

Mr. Bean wobbles back into the frame. He is dazed. He is dizzy. He turns off the camera and—

Blacked out.

chapter 6

Cock-a-doodle-doo!

With a stretch and a yawn, Mr. Bean awoke. He shook his head, rubbed his eyes, and looked around.

How had he ended up in a quaint French village?

Small, honey-colored cottages were clustered around the town square. A fountain babbled peacefully. A boy ran by, rolling a hoop with a stick. Men in berets sat outside a café. Someone played an accordion.

And a beautiful woman, a waitress, came out of the café.

Mr. Bean blinked. Where had he seen her before? Before he could figure it out—

BOOM!

A huge explosion blasted a gaping hole in the café wall!

Mr. Bean jumped up as a tank rolled into the square. A line of soldiers marched behind it.

The beautiful woman stepped in front of the tank. *"Meme quand . . ."* she began. Mr. Bean knew it was time to be a hero. He sprang into action, wrestling a soldier to the ground and taking his rifle. He knocked down a second soldier. He pushed the waitress to the ground to protect her.

"CUT!"

Mr. Bean looked up. None other than the famous Hollywood star Carson Clay was walking toward him.

And he was furious!

Behind Carson Clay, an entire film unit scrambled, terrified of his temper. "What's he doing?" screamed Clay. "And what's with his costume? Get him into something more *French*!" Without missing a beat, Carson Clay began shouting at the woman. "Sabine! You never stop speaking your line, *no matter what*!

You're crazy for the taste of Fruzzi Yogurt!"

Sabine hung her head, waiting for more of Carson Clay's wrath. Fortunately, he was distracted by a goat.

"No! No! I didn't ask for a gray goat! I asked for a white goat! A *white* goat!" Clay bellowed into a megaphone. "Will someone please get me a white goat? And a decaf latte?"

The crew scurried to satisfy Carson Clay's demands before he could think of more orders. A woman in a parka grabbed Mr. Bean's arm, mistaking him for an extra. *"T'as signé, toi?"* In French, she asked if he had signed the release form. But Mr. Bean didn't understand her.

"Tu veux êtra payé, ou pas?" She waved a wad of bills in his face as she asked if he wanted to be paid.

Mr. Bean's eyes lit up. That was *exactly* what he wanted!

A short time later, Mr. Bean was dressed

as a soldier. Carson Clay shouted directions. "You're soldiers! Terrifying soldiers who are storming the square! *ACTION!*"

Clay stared into a monitor as a tank rolled into the scene. The soldiers swarmed behind it.

But what was that flashing red light?

"CUT!" Carson Clay screamed. He ran into the square—right up to Mr. Bean, who was filming the action with his own camera! "That guy with the video camera is *fired!*"

Mr. Bean shrugged as an assistant led him away. It was time to recharge the camera's battery, anyway. He found an area full of plugs, sockets, and electrical cords, where the pyrotechnicians were setting up for the big explosion. Mr. Bean unplugged a cord so he could charge his camera.

While Mr. Bean changed into his regular clothes, Carson Clay prepared to film the big explosion scene. "Ready?" he asked. "Action!"

Once again, the tank rolled into the square. It started firing. The assistant pushed a button on the remote. But nothing blew up!

"Where's my explosion?" Carson Clay shouted. "My explosion! All I want is an explosion, a tiny little explosion! Is that too much to ask?"

During Carson Clay's tantrum, Mr. Bean sauntered back over to the electrical station. He unplugged his camera and plugged in the other cord, then turned to leave.

"Really! Is a tiny little explosion so hard for you guys? All you have to do is *this*!" the director yelled as he grabbed the remote and punched the button. He didn't know the detonator had been plugged back in.

KA-BOOM!

A huge explosion rocked the set!

And no one noticed as Mr. Bean walked away!

Mr. Bean hadn't gotten far when a shiny Mini—identical to his own—pulled up beside him. The beautiful actress who played the waitress was inside!

"Far to go?" the actress, Sabine, asked in French.

"Oui, oui!" Mr. Bean said, admiring the Mini.

"I'm going to Cannes," continued Sabine in French.

"Cannes! Cannes! Cannes!" exclaimed Mr. Bean, hopping up and down in excitement.

"Come on. Get in!" Sabine said.

As Sabine started driving, she noticed Mr. Bean's camera. "What brings you to Cannes?" she asked in French.

Mr. Bean pointed his camera out the window, then brought his fingers together to make a frame.

"Ah! You're a filmmaker, right?" Sabine asked excitedly. "I'm an artist, too. The director of that commercial is opening his film in Cannes—and I've got a part in it! Look!" She showed Mr. Bean a shiny gold ticket.

"I'm finally going to walk up the red carpet at Cannes—the dream of a lifetime!" Sabine continued, her voice choked up with emotion. Suddenly, Sabine dove beneath the seats. Mr. Bean lunged for the wheel to keep the car on the road while she dug up a box of tissues.

"I play a waitress!" Sabine said proudly as she blew her nose. But Mr. Bean just stared at her, still not understanding. Suddenly, Sabine started to cry again. "Yes! Another waitress!" She took a deep breath and sighed. "Still, it's a part. I don't see a problem with it."

Mr. Bean frowned at her, hoping she wouldn't start acting crazy again.

"No—you're right! It *is* a problem! I play nothing but waitresses—Look!" Sabine let go of the wheel again. "I can play blond waitresses . . . brunette waitresses . . . and redheaded waitresses!" She waved three wigs in the air while Mr. Bean grabbed the wheel.

Sabine grabbed his face. "Have you nothing to say to me?" she sobbed. Mr. Bean didn't have anything to say—because he didn't understand a word she was saying! But he could tell this was going to be a *long* drive.

Soon after, Mr. Bean was sitting at a table in a roadside café, surrounded by used tissues. He was thoroughly fed up.

The bathroom door opened, and Sabine, still sniffling, came out. She smiled weakly. "I'm just nervous about the premiere," she explained. "In every film I make, my scenes end up on the cutting room floor. I'm sure it will be the same this time!" Her face fell, and she rushed back to the bathroom, crying again.

Mr. Bean rolled his eyes and checked his watch. He spread his itinerary on the table and updated it again.

TOTAL TRAVEL TIME : 64 hrs

TOTAL TIME AT BEACH : 28 hrs

YIPEE DIPPY BIPPY

A television on the wall was broadcasting images of the perfect beach. Mr. Bean buried his head in his hands. Would he *ever* make it to Cannes and the beach?

Slap!

Mr. Bean looked up. Stefan was sitting across from him, grinning as he greeted Mr. Bean by slapping him. Mr. Bean was glad to see him—even if his cheek was stinging!

"There you are! You'll never believe it! I went with them!" Stefan exclaimed in Russian, pointing to the same street performers that he and Mr. Bean had seen before.

One by one, the street performers came over to Mr. Bean and tried to greet him the way Stefan did—with a slap in the face! Mr. Bean held up his hands to tell them to stop.

"They've got a cool van," Stefan continued as he mimed driving a van. "Last night we went camping and lit a fire! We had a huge meal! What did you do?"

Mr. Bean mimed his adventures for Stefan. He pretended to ride a bike. He made chicken noises. He marched like a soldier. And finally, he mimicked a woman who talked and cried all the time—just as Sabine came out of the bathroom!

"Wait till you see what I can do!" Stefan cried. The street performers started playing music—and Stefan started dancing.

Mr. Bean smiled and couldn't help but join in. Stefan was back, and things were looking better already!

Chapter 7

Soon Sabine, Stefan, and Mr. Bean were back on the road heading toward Cannes. The only problem was that each one of them spoke a different language!

"Can I keep this?" Stefan asked in Russian as he watched the video of his dance. "I want to show Papa!"

Sabine, hearing the word Papa, assumed that Mr. Bean was Stefan's dad. "It's crazy that we met up with your son like that!" she said in French.

"Is she your girlfriend?" Stefan asked Mr. Bean.

"Does this mean you're married?" Sabine asked.

"Are you going to marry her?" Stefan asked.

Mr. Bean didn't understand what they were saying to him—so he answered all their questions using his favorite French word: *"Oui!"*

Suddenly Stefan noticed Sabine's cell phone sitting next to a box of matches and a ball of yarn. "Telephone! Papa!" he cried.

Mr. Bean picked up the phone and dialed the next number on their list.

At the number he dialed, a taxi driver took a big bite of a sandwich—just before his phone rang. "'Alhggglo?" he mumbled.

Mr. Bean shook his head and disconnected. He tried the next number.

In a faraway bathroom, a man was using the toilet as his cell phone rang. He tried to answer it, but the phone fell into the toilet!

Mr. Bean shrugged and hung up. They weren't making any progress.

Sabine drove for hours, long after the sun

had set. Stefan curled up in the backseat and fell asleep. Even Mr. Bean yawned and shut his eyes—just for a moment . . .

BEEEEEEEEP!

A blaring horn jolted Mr. Bean awake. Sabine had fallen asleep, too—with her face pressed against the horn. But the Mini was still driving along!

Mr. Bean grabbed the wheel and turned it sharply. The car spun in a complete circle before it was heading in the right direction again. Mr. Bean looked at Sabine, who was snoring quietly. He smiled, very satisfied with his new plan. Within minutes, Sabine was asleep in the passenger seat, and Mr. Bean was speeding along the dark highway to Cannes!

But after a few hours, Mr. Bean started to fall asleep, too. His head dropped onto the wheel, just as Sabine's had. Mr. Bean shook himself awake. He *had* to keep driving—no matter how tired he was. He slapped his cheeks. He chomped on his hand. He would do anything to stay focused on the drive.

But his tired eyes still began to blur. The letters on the French sign before him seemed to rearrange before his very eyes. ATTENTION À TA VITESSE became YOU'LL NEVER MAKE IT. Even the road signs were against him!

BEEEEEEEP!

BEEEEEEEEEEEEEEEEEEEEEP!

Mr. Bean snapped awake just in time to swerve out of the way of a huge truck! He looked frantically around the Mini. Surely there was something he could do to stay awake. If only he could come up with a plan . . .

A smug grin spread across his face. Of course he could come up with a plan—he was Mr. Bean! And with the box of matches and the yarn close at hand, he knew exactly how to handle this situation.

Hours later, sunlight streamed through the Mini. Morning had arrived at last. Sabine yawned and stretched as she awoke. In the distance, the blue waves crashed upon the beach.

"We made it!" Sabine shrieked. She turned to Mr. Bean, who had propped his eyelids open with matchsticks and tied his hands to the steering wheel with yarn. "You did it! You're fantastic!"

"The sea! I can see the sea!" yelled Stefan when he woke. He grabbed Mr. Bean's camera so he could film their arrival.

The glorious blue sea crashing onto soft yellow sand. Sabine sticks her head out the sunroof. Mr. Bean smiles. Sabine plants a kiss on his cheek. Mr. Bean wrinkles his nose and wipes off the kiss. The film jostles as Mr. Bean takes the camera. He films Stefan. He films Sabine. Sabine grabs his wrist.

"Look at the time! It's not possible. The premiere starts in half an hour!" Sabine gasped. She ran back to the Mini and hurtled herself into the backseat. "Hurry! Hurry! You drive!"

Stefan and Mr. Bean jumped into the car as Sabine pulled on a dress from the pile of clothes in the backseat. Mr. Bean stepped on the gas pedal. They didn't go far before the Mini started making some odd noises. **Sput-sput-sput-sputtttttt.**

The car was out of gas!

"Oh, no!" moaned Sabine.

But Mr. Bean was one step ahead of her. He could already see a gas station. He steered the sputtering Mini up to a pump. Sabine dashed into the bathroom to finish getting ready.

A woman at the next pump looked at Mr. Bean. Her eyes grew wide. It was almost as if she recognized Mr. Bean from somewhere. She jumped into her car and zoomed off.

While Mr. Bean finished pumping the gas, Sabine emerged from the bathroom, ready for the premiere. She glanced at a blaring TV and saw Mr. Bean on the news!

". . . as pictures of the Englishman believed to have abducted Jury Member Emil Dachevsky's son were released, a positive ID of the boy was made yesterday, and police believe the kidnapper is now traveling with an accomplice," announced the reporter.

Sabine's mouth dropped open as a fuzzy photo of herself appeared on the broadcast!

"A national manhunt has been launched and security tightened around the Festival," continued the reporter. But Sabine missed the rest of the report. She was already running to the Mini!

"You are not Russian filmmaker?" she asked in accented English.

"Non," replied Mr. Bean.

"You are not this boy's father?" she continued.

"Non!" Mr. Bean said.

"You are English?" demanded Sabine.

"Oui," replied Mr. Bean.

"You say nothing but *oui* and *non*?" Sabine snapped.

"Gracias!" Mr. Bean said, trying to be helpful.

"Stop saying *gracias*!" Sabine yelled. "The whole of France look for you! Now they look for me, too! Who are you? Why are you in France? Where are you going?"

"To the beach," Mr. Bean said simply. He showed Sabine his itinerary. When she looked at his homemade map and saw the eagerness in his face, she knew that he hadn't kidnapped Stefan. Besides, if he *had* kidnapped Stefan, why would the boy have been so happy to see Mr. Bean? Why would he have jumped into the car with them?

Sabine revved the engine and zoomed away.

"It was only on TV for a moment," she said reassuringly. "Perhaps no one will recognize your face."

Just at that moment, the Mini passed an entire wall of Wanted posters—with Mr. Bean's face on them! They were posted right next to Missing posters with Stefan's picture.

"When we get to Cannes, we will return the

boy to his father. You will go to the beach, and I will go to the premiere," Sabine continued. She sounded like she was in total control—until a police roadblock appeared before them! "Police! Oh, no! What are we going to do? I don't know what to do!"

Stefan leaned forward and gave Sabine a quick slap to the cheek. It was just what she needed to stop panicking.

"I know *exactly* what to do," she said, full of determination.

Minutes later, the Mini pulled up to the roadblock.

"Bonjour, madame," the officer said.

"Bonjour," Sabine replied with a wide, charming smile. She gestured at the backseat, where Stefan was wearing a pink punk wig and sunglasses. "My son—they grow up so fast!"

The policeman grinned back at her.

"And this is my mother," Sabine continued. She pointed to Mr. Bean, who was dressed as a lady—a very old lady, in a white wig, a dress, lipstick, and earrings!

"Bonjour, madame," the policeman repeated.

"Gracias!" replied Mr. Bean.

"She's Spanish," Sabine quickly said.

The flirty policeman smiled again.

"Buenas días, señora!"

"And profoundly deaf!" Sabine announced. "Sir, we're in a great hurry. I don't want to miss my premiere . . ."

"I'm sorry, madam. I didn't know," the policeman said in French. "We will accompany you there!"

And that was how the Mini pulled up at the red carpet surrounded by policemen on motorcycles. The police lights were flashing, but the cops didn't realize that the demure old lady in the car was the fugitive they were hunting!

Sabine turned to Stefan. "Come with me. We find your papa and—"

A security guard interrupted her. *"Billets, s'il vous plaît!"*

Sabine handed him her ticket. But the guard shook his head. "One only," he replied in French. He turned to Stefan. "You stay here with Grandma."

"No!" cried Sabine. "He's my son!"

But the guard wouldn't budge.

Mr. Bean and Stefan would have to stay outside—surrounded by the police!

Chapter 8

Nervously, Sabine walked the red carpet. She glanced back at the Mini, but there was nothing she could do to bring Stefan with her. Inside the auditorium, she took a seat among the glamorous people, including Carson Clay and Stefan's parents.

The lights dimmed. The music swelled. In the darkness, Carson Clay's voice rang out as the film began. "What is life? A teardrop in the eye of infinity . . ."

Sabine rolled her eyes. She hoped that she wouldn't be bored to tears while she waited for her scene.

Outside the auditorium, Mr. Bean and Stefan were also bored. Very bored. Mr. Bean figured that they might as well *try* to get into the auditorium.

After stowing his camera in a large handbag, Mr. Bean took Stefan's hand and tottered on high heels to the back entrance. A burly security guard sat at a desk listening to classical music. Mr. Bean remembered the way he and Stefan had acted out *O Mio Babbino Caro*. It had worked perfectly before—and he had a feeling it would again!

The guard glanced up as a very strange-looking woman—Mr. Bean in disguise—staggered toward him, carrying a kid wearing a crazy wig. "No entry! What's going on?" the guard barked in French.

"Ugggghhhhh," groaned Stefan, pretending to be very sick. Mr. Bean laid him on the ground and wept. The guard started to look worried. What if there was something really wrong with the kid?

And that's when Mr. Bean walloped the

guard with his handbag and knocked him out! Stefan raced down the hallway with Mr. Bean wobbling behind him as another guard approached.

Mr. Bean and Stefan slipped through a heavy black curtain and found themselves behind the giant screen playing Carson Clay's movie. They tore off their disguises and peeked out at the audience.

"Papa! Mama!" whispered Stefan excitedly. He showed Mr. Bean where his parents were sitting. Mr. Bean smiled. He patted a nearby chair, telling Stefan to wait there until the film was over so that he would have time to escape.

And then it was time to say good-bye. Mr. Bean gave Stefan a little wave and turned to go.

But Stefan ran after him. He reached out and gently slapped Mr. Bean on the cheek. Mr. Bean returned the slap. He slipped out the door—only to find that the two guards from backstage were at the end of the hall!

Mr. Bean slunk back into the auditorium,

but another security guard was patrolling the opposite aisle. Three more guards were gathered in the back, whispering into their headsets. Mr. Bean had to stay out of sight. He ducked under a row of seats and shimmied along the floor until he reached Sabine. He tapped her foot.

"What! How did you—the boy! He is with his father?" she gasped. Mr. Bean held a finger to his lips as a guard paused at their row.

"Look!" Sabine whispered urgently. "My scene!" They watched the screen as Carson Clay's character walked into an empty French restaurant. In the background stood Sabine.

"I keep coming back to our place, hoping to see you. If only I could talk to someone!" the actor said. In the film, Sabine took a step toward him. She opened her mouth.

And suddenly, the scene cut to Carson Clay leaving the restaurant!

"No!" howled Sabine in horror. "They cut my scene! They cut my scene!" As she burst into tears, people turned to look at her. Mr. Bean dove beneath the seats. By the time Sabine looked down, he was gone.

Click. Click. Click. The shiny shoes of a guard tapped as he patrolled the aisle. When he passed, Mr. Bean popped his head out from beneath a ball gown. He climbed into the aisle and tried to casually walk toward the exit.

Then the guard turned around and started back down the aisle. Mr. Bean was trapped! He ran to the back of the auditorium. But two more guards were heading his way!

Mr. Bean pressed himself against the wall. Just then, a door in the wall opened. The projectionist was sneaking out for a break! Mr. Bean dashed into the tiny projection room. He peeked out the window to see what was going on in the auditorium.

Suddenly, a man's voice behind him boomed, "Put your hands in the air."

Mr. Bean's eyes popped open. He was done for! He threw his arms into the air, hoping the authorities would go easy on him if he behaved.

"Move away from the door," continued the man. Again, Mr. Bean obeyed.

"And drop the gun!" commanded the man.

Mr. Bean dropped an imaginary gun. Then he realized—he didn't have a gun! The voice was from the film's sound track!

Mr. Bean breathed a sigh of relief and looked around the projection room. He was the only person there. Along one wall, a filmstrip zigzagged through dozens of bobbins before being projected through a small window. There was also a video projector, but it wasn't in use. Mr. Bean looked out the window again. In the audience, he could see that Sabine was still crying. He turned to leave the room and—hopefully—make it to the beach before being caught.

Then he stopped. A smile spread across his face.

Mr. Bean had an idea.

He plugged his camera into the video projector. When he rewound the tape in his camera, a blur of images appeared on the movie screen. Carson Clay bolted up in his seat. By the time he glared at the projection room, his film was playing normally again.

Until an image of Sabine outside the *Gare du Nord*—that Mr. Bean had filmed—appeared!

Sabine stared at the screen in amazement. Where was this new film coming from?

Mr. Bean switched back to Carson Clay's film. "Without you I am nothing, and the world is nothing . . ." the actor moaned on-screen.

Then his film was replaced by Mr. Bean's video again. Sabine stood in the quaint town square, filming the Fruzzi Yogurt commercial. In the soft, golden light, she looked beautiful.

And in the auditorium, she couldn't believe her eyes!

Mr. Bean was having a grand time. He peeked out the window at the overjoyed Sabine and felt that he'd done a fine job in cheering her up. He was about to pack up his camera when he heard this on the sound track:

"How can I live, knowing that you've found another man?" Carson Clay despaired.

A mischievous smile spread across Mr. Bean's face. How could he resist a line like that?

Carson Clay's voice-overs continued as Mr. Bean played specific scenes from his home movie.

"I know what he'll be like. His own man . . ."

Film of Mr. Bean stuffing an entire lobster in his mouth. Even the claws are hanging out!

"You'll have gone for a guy that's a little conservative . . ."

Film of Mr. Bean dressed as an invading soldier, marching in the square.

"But he'll know how to make you happy . . ."

Film of Mr. Bean wiggling his hips and shaking his shoulders to "Mr. Boombastic."

Mr. Bean grinned as he watched the massive

image of himself dancing. Behind the movie screen, Stefan stood on his chair and danced along!

Now it was really time for Mr. Bean to get going. He unplugged his video camera to let Carson Clay's movie resume, accidentally leaning against the filmstrip to reach the cord.

SN-A-A-A-A-P!

The film broke in two!

Mr. Bean watched in horror as the two ends of the film zipped away in opposite directions. He lunged for one and leaped for the other. With fumbling hands he tied the pieces of film into a thick double knot. He crossed his fingers and hoped for the best.

At first, everything seemed fine as Carson Clay's voice rang out, saying, "I come here each night hoping to find you . . ." But when the knotted part of the film reached the projector, it jammed in the machine! The picture froze, and the sound died.

Mr. Bean had to think fast. He plugged

his camera in again, hit play, and turned the volume up to high.

An image of Sabine lights up the screen. She is back in the quaint village square, her arms outstretched, in a pose both beautiful and heartbreaking. The tragic opera song "O Mio Babbino Caro" that Mr. Bean and Stefan had pantomimed echoes through the auditorium.

The audience was captivated. No one looked away from the screen, except for Carson Clay, who finally got up and charged off to the projection booth. But by that point, Mr. Bean had stopped thinking about the audience. He was too busy with the film—which had started to smoke!

In seconds, the filmstrip burst into flames. Mr. Bean frantically fed half of it into the projector, but the other end of the film started to pile up on the floor. He had to maintain the filmstrip's tension so that the movie would still play! He started coiling the film around his legs to keep it tight.

Outside, Carson Clay ordered a guard to break down the door. Mr. Bean looked up in panic as the guard slammed his body against the door. But the sturdy lock didn't budge.

The projectionist returned from his break. "What's going on?" he asked.

"Open the door!" roared Carson Clay. The projectionist pulled a key from his pocket and put it in the lock.

Mr. Bean heard the key in the lock. He had to escape, but it wasn't going to be easy now that he was wrapped up with film! He hopped toward the other door, leaving his camera running.

WHAM! The door burst open, and Carson Clay, the projectionist, and the guard stormed into the room—just in time to see the end of the filmstrip trail out the door. Carson Clay grabbed the strip and pulled it hard.

At the top of the stairs, Mr. Bean was yanked backward. He toppled over and rolled down the stairs, unwinding the filmstrip as he fell. Carson Clay, the guards, and the projectionist raced to the stairs. But when they got there, all they could see was a mound of film at the bottom of the stairwell. Mr. Bean had disappeared.

They didn't notice him slip back into the projection room, blocking the door with a chair!

On the screen, Carson Clay's film zoomed in for a close-up of his eye. Meanwhile, Mr. Bean's movie played an image of Sabine over Carson Clay's eyeball. The audience was captivated by the beautiful actress.

There was more frantic banging at the door. When the guard forced it open, Carson Clay charged into the room—but Mr. Bean had disappeared again!

"Where is he now?" yelled Carson Clay. Then he and the projectionist saw Mr. Bean's face peeping in through the tiny projection window.

Mr. Bean was hanging outside of the projection room—his feet dangling high above the audience!

"I'm going to kill you!" bellowed Carson Clay. But Mr. Bean was too quick for him. He dropped into the back row of the audience. There were guards in the aisle to his right. And more guards—and Carson Clay—in the aisle to his left. There was only one way out for Mr. Bean: right down the middle, over the heads of the audience!

There were too many people sitting in the rows for the guards to reach Mr. Bean. And when one tried, Sabine was quick to trip him.

Up in the projection room, the projectionist desperately tried to save Carson Clay's film. The sound was working, but Mr. Bean's movie was still playing. The film of his adventures— and misadventures—flickered across the screen at top speed: the train, Stefan, Sabine . . . and Mr. Bean and Sabine, overlooking the glorious beaches of Cannes.

Mr. Bean's movie came to an end. The image

paused on Mr. Bean and Sabine as Carson Clay's voice said, "It is that most precious of all things—it is friendship." Music swelled as Carson Clay's film ended, too.

Mr. Bean jumped off the seats and ran up to the stage.

"He stole my son!" Emil shouted as he jumped to his feet. Emil raced up to the stage. "Where is he? Where is my son?"

The projectionist was still struggling with Mr. Bean's camera. An image of Stefan in front of the view of Cannes froze on the screen—just as the real Stefan hopped off his seat and walked onto the stage. The audience watched in shock as the guards approached Mr. Bean.

"No!" Stefan cried. "He is my friend!"

Mr. Bean stared at Stefan, his mouth open wide. "You speak *English*?" he asked.

"Of course!" Stefan replied with a mischievous grin.

There was a moment of silence. Then the audience members rose to their feet. They burst into applause. Stefan ran to his parents.

People rushed to Sabine to shake her hand and congratulate her. Laughing and smiling, she searched for Mr. Bean in the crowd.

She found him sitting on the stairs, with his camera in his lap and his itinerary in his hands. Once again, Mr. Bean updated it:

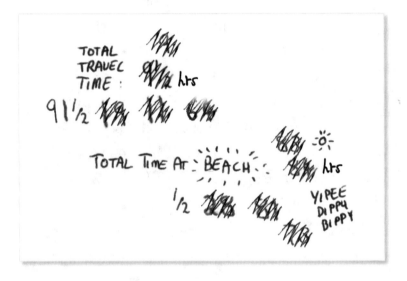

Only one half hour—thirty short minutes—to spend at the beach. But Mr. Bean hadn't traveled so far, and been through so much, to give up now.

At the far side of the stage, a door swung

open. Just beyond it, the clear blue ocean shimmered in the sun.

Mr. Bean couldn't take his eyes off the beach. He *wouldn't* take his eyes off it—not until he was sitting on the warm sand. He walked out the door onto the edge of a flat roof—and stepped off the side!

Fortunately, a truck was stopped at a traffic light, creating the perfect step-down for Mr. Bean. And next to the truck was a smaller truck that Mr. Bean stepped on. The next step down was onto a car, then onto an ice-cream cart, then onto a cart filled with beach chairs, and then onto the back of a moped. The vehicles formed the perfect staircase!

Mr. Bean stepped onto the beach. He opened the top button of his shirt. He kicked off his shoes. He pulled off his socks. He picked up a handful of sand and let it run through his fingers.

At last!

But Mr. Bean wasn't enjoying the beach alone. With a little help from his new friends

Sabine and Stefan, Mr. Bean built a sand castle in the shape of his Mini car. Stefan's parents built a sand castle, too, along with the movie projectionist. Even Carson Clay built one.

And not far away, the policemen from the roadblock and the security guards from the auditorium played Frisbee. Even the street performers were at the beach, playing an exciting game of cricket!

Mr. Bean sighed happily as he wiggled his toes in the sand. It hadn't exactly been the peaceful, restful vacation he'd imagined.

It had been even better!